T0361460

The
KEEPER
of the
ORNAMENTS

McSWEENEY'S
SAN FRANCISCO

Cover illustration by Angel Chang.

ISBN: 978-1-963270-00-6

Not sure what these numbers mean but here goes:
10 9 8 7 6 5 4 3 2 1

www.mcsweeneys.net

Printed in Canada

The

KEEPER

of the

ORNAMENTS

by

DAVE EGGERS

McSWEENEY'S

For DWC, and half a century of friendship

COLE GOT HOME, emptied his pockets of keys and phone, and went to his bedroom to change out of his work clothes. He was standing in his boxers when he heard the voices and the thunder of manic feet. Someone was in the unit next door. The volume was astonishing. It was somehow louder than if the people were in his own apartment.

The adjoining unit, a mirror image of his own, had been empty as long as he'd lived in the building. Two years ago, there had been a murder-suicide in the unit, and even after Sheila, Cole's landlord, changed the unit's number, from 4A to 3½, any internet search quickly led to lurid stories and photos of the blood-stained walls. Whenever Cole talked to Sheila, she asked him if he had friends who might want 3½. She could offer a discount.

Cole did not have friends like that. His friends were far away, in Memphis, where he'd gone to college, and they called less and less as the years went on. He was forty-four, lived alone, and was dating no one. He was a logistics expert for a shipping company, worked largely on his own, and had become indispensable to a company that seemed to lay off a fourth of its staff every six months. Once a week he played in a surprisingly serious over-forty bocce league, for which he'd become the commissioner. His life did not resemble the one he'd envisioned.

Sheila had told him nothing about a new tenant, so he was inclined to think the apartment was being shown to an especially loud family who would soon be gone. He changed into his basketball shorts and sweatshirt and went to the kitchen. There was the shrieking of girls. There was the thunder of feet running up and down the stairs. Someone dropped a plate and the crash was three-dimensional; it exploded inside his head.

He stepped out his front door, thinking he might find the door to 3½ open—maybe the realtor had left it open during the showing?—but the door was closed.

He went back inside and waited. The visit couldn't last more than fifteen minutes. He warmed up his taquitos and cut a bell pepper and sprinkled the plate with basil leaves and ate standing up at the kitchen counter. All the while, the noise next door gusted from one room to another like a tropical storm. There seemed to be a herd of children, six or ten of them, crashing into furniture and flinging themselves into walls. There was an older voice, also female, that he guessed was the mother's. He heard no other voices, no second adult voice that might be the realtor's.

Fifteen minutes went by. Cole ate, cleaned his plate and put it in the dishwasher. The voices remained and grew more excited. The possibility that they might be new tenants hit him with terrible force.

He would have to move. Even one night of this would drive him mad. The building had always been silent. He'd never heard a noise that wasn't his own. The woman below him was in her eighties and barely moved. The unit diagonally down shared no walls with his, and was occupied by a graduate student from Beijing, an architect. They'd said hello a few times, and Cole had once seen an intricate model in the dumpster. It was gorgeous, white like a city of crystal, and he'd wanted to save it, bring it to his apartment, wanted to ask her about it. But he didn't feel right salvaging what she'd planned to destroy. And after that she'd all but disappeared.

By ten o'clock the noise had subsided. The children had gone to bed, he surmised. But then the TV came on, so loud he heard every word.

He stepped onto the shared back balcony. Without effort he could stand on his deck, and with a leftward glance see the main room of 3½ through its sliding glass doors. The apartment looked largely empty, but in a folding beach chair facing a TV, there was a young woman sitting upright, the remote control held limply in her hand. He stepped quickly back into his apartment. If they were indeed new neighbors, he couldn't be introduced this way. He heard the distant wail of a coyote, and taking this as a cue, he retreated to his living room.

But now he seemed to be sharing his living room with his neighbor; the wall between them was meaningless. She was watching a show with a laugh track, and every squeal and wave of applause reverberated through his apartment. It was too soon to ask her to turn the volume down, too soon to make trouble with a new neighbor unwinding after a trying day. He brushed his teeth, knowing that if they were his new neighbors, there was nothing he could do but find another place to live. He could not ask children not to be children. The fault was in the construction itself. The building was so cheap, the walls so thin. He lay in bed and thought about where he might go.

But then they were gone. When he returned from work the next afternoon, 3½ was silent. And it was silent the next night, too. By the end of the week he was sure it had been some anomalous event. Maybe they were friends of Sheila's who needed the place for a night. Or could it be that 3½ was now a homeshare?

In any case the week was quiet and Cole felt a vaulting joy that left him restless. He went to the company gym, something he did once or twice a year, and he lifted free weights furiously, did crunches with his arms crossed like a penitent, and jogged on the treadmill for half an hour while watching a scene of what appeared to be a forest in Eastern Europe. He slept better than usual, and deeply, and dreamt strangely, and slept so long on Saturday that it was the noise of a truck, at half past ten, that woke him. The rattling opening of the rolling door was loud enough that it seemed to be in his bedroom, in his skull. He walked to the front door and saw a moving truck with half a rainbow painted across its side. A small uniformed man was carrying a red leather chair over his head, and the same woman he'd seen a week before was leading him.

Cole closed his door quickly and stood, stunned, in his foyer. Again he thought of where he might go. Maybe it was time to move back to Memphis, to be a kind of uncle to the children of his college friends. He got their Christmas cards and thought he could enter their lives, create a calendar of birthdays, be the thoughtful and extravagant friend who was never more than ten minutes away.

His father, his reinvented father, would invite him to stay at his new farm near the Oregon border. At seventy-six, he had remarried, to a woman of sixty named Melanie, and though they had plenty of space—a whole guesthouse, newly remodeled—Cole would not burden them. When Cole was growing up, his father had been an intermittently employed welder with a booming voice when drunk, cut with sarcasm and a tendency to accuse his wife and two sons of minor crimes—denting the car, unplugging the fridge. Every night brought a three-act drama, his mother roaring hoarsely in her defense and her sons', but she had no appetite for the fight. They divorced when Cole and his brother were teens, she died at fifty-eight, and now his father was a gregarious and sober man of leisure. He'd met Melanie at AA, and was now a sought-after sponsor. They had three dogs.

The sane who escape loud childhoods seek out quiet, cultivate quiet, but the noise on the neighbors' moving day was unlike anything he'd thought possible. It sounded like a series of air strikes. Each time the door closed, the building shook. The movers thumped up the outside steps, the inside staircase. They hammered and drilled and pounded furniture into place. And finally, at six, he heard a doorbell. Instinctively he went to it, but it was the neighbors'. They had installed a new one and it was a clamorous chiming—ascending notes, each of them increasingly desperate. They'd ordered pizza and he could smell it as distinctly as if he were eating it himself, under his bedcovers.

The rest of the night was worse. There was singing. There was more shrieking. His best guess was that there were four or five girls, all under ten. At some point there was a fight between them. The stairs rumbled and a door slammed. And finally there were the footsteps of an adult going upstairs. Cole looked at his watch; it was just after ten. This was bedtime for them, it seemed. He wondered if there was any way he could live with this. He would eat out more. He would eat out or see a movie, get home at nine, have an hour of cacophony and then quiet.

But the footsteps traveled downstairs and the TV thrummed awake—now louder, though, than the sitcom from earlier in the week. This show involved screaming and crashing. How did the children sleep through this? He did not sleep through it. Between the noise next door and working out his plans to leave the building, by dawn he'd slept no more than an hour.

In the gray morning, a manic rattling began. He first assumed it was the kids. But it was too crazed, metallic. He guessed it was a raccoon. They got into the dumpster in the alley and often couldn't get out. He rolled over to see that it was 6:34. He walked into the kitchen and saw nothing. From his back deck, he looked down into the alleyway and saw nothing.

A bang sounded, then a circular swish of pots and pans. The noise was coming from the kitchen cabinets. He thought again of a raccoon. He grabbed a broom and inched toward the sound. His first thought was that he might convince the animal to exit the way it had entered. So Cole took the broom and rapped the cabinet door with it, hoping it might scare the animal into retreat. But the result was tenfold chaos; the animal went into a terrified panic and vastly expanded the area of its noisemaking. The lower cabinet was connected from the corner all the way to the sink, so the animal clanged and scratched from one end to the other and back.

Containment, Cole thought, and found the duct tape. He taped the five doors of the lower cabinets closed; the animal was better in there than in his apartment. With the doors shut, Cole made coffee and sat at the bar, with a view of the cabinets. There were stretches of furious activity, when the animal rushed around and even threw itself against the doors, and these were followed by minutes of what he assumed was quiet planning.

His doorbell rang. Cole looked at the time: 6:46.

He opened the door to find his new neighbor. Her hair was black, shoulder-length, streaked with pink. Her eyes were dark, her face oval and unwrinkled. If he'd had to guess, he would have said she had one Asian parent, one Caucasian. She was slightly taller and heavier than Cole, wearing a long ribbed sweater dress and a string of white pearls. She was very young, probably no more than thirty, he thought. Then she smiled—an easy and toothy and tired smile. "I know this sounds strange," she said, "but I think our cat is in your cabinet."

She looked toward his kitchen just as the rattle of the animal began again. He let her in. "I'm Daphne, by the way," she said, moving quickly past him, following the sound. She crouched down at the cabinet door. "Duct tape. Okay, I get it. Can I?" She mimed the removal of the tape. Cole shrugged.

She removed one key strip, opened the cabinet door, and a champagne-colored blur bounded out, leaping over Daphne's shoulder and into the living room. It was a cat—a rope-muscled cat with a long neck and pointy pink-lined ears.

Daphne sat on her behind on the kitchen floor, and watched the cat race manically through the apartment. She made no move to capture or contain it. Then, using the flashlight on her phone, she investigated the cabinet. "Apparently there's a door between the two cabinets, yours and ours. Were you aware?"

Cole had had no clue.

"Come look," she said, and Cole knelt next to her. She smelled of a powdery deodorant and something else. Bacon. She'd just made bacon.

With her phone's flashlight, she helped him see that behind the pots and pans, in the far corner of the cabinet, there was a crude opening in the drywall, with a plastic flap attached at the top.

"I'm guessing at some point this was built to allow someone's cat, or maybe a dog, to go between the two places?" she said. "And maybe they built it where the landlord wouldn't see?"

"But it requires you to keep the cabinets open," Cole said.

"Maybe just ajar," Daphne said, and Cole was struck by the word. *Ajar.* It wasn't a word you often heard spoken aloud.

They stood up, and Cole found the cat sharpening its claws on the arm of his couch. Daphne rushed over, yelling, "Hey! Hey!," though this only caused the cat to speed up its work. She grabbed the animal under its belly and lifted. Its claws were deeply embedded, so she had to pull it, like a piece of taffy, until it gave way. "Sorry," she said, and brought the cat to Cole. It looked up at him with sea-green eyes. "This is Anders." Cole waved hello. She dropped Anders on the floor and the cat attacked a nearby plant.

He poured Daphne a cup of coffee. "We just moved in," she said. "I guess that was obvious. I'm sorry about the noise. Was it loud?"

Cole tilted his head back and forth.

"So it was loud," she said. "We try not to be."

"Thin walls," Cole said.

"We're from Nevada. You'll meet the girls," she said. "Savannah and June."

Two girls, Cole thought. Could there really be only two?

"Just you here?" she asked, and suddenly she focused all her acuity on him.

"Just me," he said, and her eyes registered the briefest concern before she turned away and blew on her coffee. She took in the apartment.

"I'm thinking of moving," he said.

"Oh? Why?" she asked.

"Work. The commute," he said vaguely.

"But Anders already seems to like you," she said. Anders had shown no interest in Cole at all, but he appreciated her kindness. He liked her. She had manners, the sort of manners he'd grown up with. Introductions, apologies, acceptance of coffee, interest in one's host. She would be a good neighbor, he figured, if not for the thin walls and the cat door. On cue, a new rattling came from the cabinet, and a second cat, much like the first, emerged.

"That's Fernando," Daphne said, nodding at him as he bounded toward Cole's bedroom. "Anders's brother."

This second cat's fur was coarser, messier, and while Anders's eyes were green, Fernando's were blue. Fernando soon found Anders and they chased each

13

other around Cole's apartment like molecules in a particle collider. Cole was sure something would break, or Daphne would gather them apologetically and leave, but neither happened. Then a new sound came through the walls. "Mama?"

"That's the girls," Daphne said. "Just waking up. I should go. Thanks for this," she said, and brought her coffee cup to the sink, washed it out and set it on the dish rack.

She made her way to the door before turning back to get the cats. Cole didn't think one person could gather both, given that one was now on the head of his leather chair and the other on the kitchen counter, inspecting his juicer. But in seconds Daphne had them both in her hands, like lumps of wet pasta, and at the doorway she said she and her girls would have Cole over sometime.

"So the cat door, we should block it?" she asked.

"Might as well. For now," Cole said.

A few days later, in the early evening, there was a knock at his door. He looked through the peephole and saw that it was Daphne. The two girls were with her.

"Cole," he said, and put his hand on his chest.

"Right," Daphne said. "We thought you should meet everyone. Want to come over for tea? We just got back from the grocery store."

He followed them into their apartment, a twin to his own. Their furniture was bright, upholstered with a mix of patterns and primary colors, and an array of potted plants led to the back porch, where another half dozen were taking in the last minutes of sun. In the living room, three moving boxes were stacked, and a tall pile of folded laundry was tilting dramatically on the second step of the carpeted stairway.

Daphne began putting the groceries away. "This is Savannah. She's eight," she said, and pointed to a girl in pink, missing her two front teeth and wearing furry slippers with unicorn horns extending from the front toes. She half hid behind her mother. The shy one, Cole assumed.

"And this is Junie. June. She's nine." June, in a denim jacket and pajama pants, placed her hands under her chin and struck a catalog pose. The ham, Cole thought.

"We're still moving in," Daphne said, folding one

of the empty grocery bags. She stuffed it into the crack between the top of the refrigerator and the cabinet above. That's where Cole's mom had always put them. As if realizing the party was in the kitchen, the cats emerged from upstairs and chased each other around the tiled floor.

"Mama, what're we eating?" June asked.

"We're eating Thai noodles. I told you in the store. And on the way home. And as we were getting out of the car. We'll make them together. Green or black?" she asked Cole, holding two boxes of Lipton. He chose green.

"But you told the guy at the store you can't cook," June said.

Daphne smiled at Cole. "I was just bantering. There are things we say in small talk, and then there's the truth." She turned to Cole. "Right, Mr. Cole?"

"Right," Cole said, and believed this to be true.

"Do you know which cat is which yet?" Savannah asked. She was holding both cats like droopy barbells. Anders and Fernando allowed themselves to be regarded for a moment before squirming free and dropping to the ground with two quick thumps.

"I'm not sure," Cole lied. "Help me."

Daphne handed him a cup, the tea bag's string dangling from the lip.

"Fernando has blue eyes and Anders's are green. And Fernando has brown in his face," Savannah said. She opened the freezer and pulled out a popsicle.

"Not now. You know that," Daphne said.

Savannah put the popsicle back without argument. "Do you know which one is faster?" she asked Cole.

"I don't. Could it be Anders?" Cole said.

"He *looks* faster, but it's actually Fernando," Savannah said. "Fernando's not as smart, though. He's the one who eats soup, then pukes."

"Are you married?" June asked.

"I told you he isn't," Daphne said to her. "Sorry," she said to Cole.

"I'm not. Do you think I should get married?" he asked June. "I'd never thought about it until just now."

He saw Daphne smile to herself, as if he'd managed a borderline joke just right. Daphne reminded him so much of his own mother, and his own mother's way of parenting, that he was momentarily struck dumb. She seemed a reincarnation.

"Their dad lives in Nevada," Daphne said. "We're separated. He's a…" She faked a smile. "He's getting remarried."

Cole hoped there was nothing expected of him there. He didn't know what to say. I hope to meet him someday? In the silence, Savannah seemed to notice the unsure moment. She squared her body to him and said, "Well, you should probably get back to your apartment."

"Savannah! That's not how we talk to guests," Daphne said.

"He's our *neighbor*," Savannah said. "There's a difference." She picked up Fernando, threw him over her shoulder, and disappeared into the downstairs bedroom, likely Daphne's. June followed.

"Sorry," Daphne said. The top button on her blouse was undone, and after she saw him notice it, she fixed it while pretending to play with her necklace.

"I won't ever hit on you," he said suddenly.

She looked up at him. "I didn't—" She couldn't find the words. Finally she smiled. "That's very kind of you."

"Daphne, I am in my forties," he said, and discovered that he was suddenly speaking in a formal, clipped tone. "And I have romantic interests outside this building. I'm guessing you're in your twenties?"

"Just thirty," she said.

"I date people my own age," he said. "And I would never make your residence here more difficult or complicated."

"Thank you. I appreciate that," she said. "I actually do. No one's ever said that to me before, and if you mean it, that's very kind of you."

"I do mean it," he said.

"Like, I could see it being a reverse-psychology sort of come-on."

"I thought of that, too. I'm not many things, but I am consistent," Cole said. "If you ask me a question today, and ask me the same question five years from now, the answer will be the same. People have told me that."

"I can't imagine what question I'd ask you today and five years from now, but the point is taken. You consistently are not interested in me romantically. Not now or five years from now."

Cole sighed.

"I'm kidding," she said. "But seriously. Thank you." Cole's relief was enormous.

"And I've never been accused or convicted of any crime," he said. "Many years ago, to be a hockey coach, I submitted to an FBI background check, and I was clean. I still am clean. I want you to feel at ease."

"I do. I did, and now I'm even more so. And FBI check. Got it. Wow."

A week later, the bell rang. Through the peephole he saw that it was June and Savannah.

"Hold on," he said, and went to his kitchen counter.

He'd ordered a cardigan, thinking it might hint at him being more of a grandfatherly presence. He opened the shipping box, put on the cardigan, and answered the door. The girls seemed to register some difference in him, but they said nothing.

Savannah handed him a business envelope, what appeared to be a repurposed statement from the Bank of America. In the address window they'd written the word PROPOSEL.

"Should I open it now?" Cole asked.

"No, wait till we're gone!" June said, and they scrambled back to their apartment.

Cole sat in his wingback chair and unfolded the letter. It outlined a plan for reopening what they called the Trans-Apartment Cat Tunnel. Cole suspected that Daphne had helped with the document, but it was written in a child's hand and was full of misspellings and grammatical innovations. The idea had clearly originated with the girls.

In their apartment, they wrote, the cats regularly meowed in the direction of the cabinet, and were generally curious and seeking out new things to see and do. But because they were indoor cats, they couldn't be allowed to roam the neighborhood. So the girls were proposing certain times of day when the cabinet's tunnel would be open. "Tolls are optional," the proposal said. On the other side of the page there was a question, followed by boxes labeled YES and NO. "Do you agree with this proposel?" it asked. "Mark your answer and return to Apartment 3½ ASAP!"

Cole had no earthly interest in letting the cats into his apartment. He'd never had pets, did not want pets, but he did not want to disappoint the girls.

Cole marked "Yes" and thought the girls would appreciate more cloak-and-dagger, so he taped the envelope to their front door, knocked, and retreated to his own apartment before they could see him.

Five minutes later he heard the clatter of pots and pans, and opened the cabinet door to catch the blur of Fernando and Anders, who burst into his kitchen like shoppers who'd been waiting since dawn for a Thanksgiving sale.

That first week of the opening of the Trans-Apartment Cat Tunnel, Cole learned many things. One was that anything that could be knocked over was knocked over, and usually it was intentional. These cats were impossibly elegant and nimble, able to balance on the lip of a windowsill. They could leap four feet without effort, and could weave between a dozen glasses without so much as stirring any one of them. And yet, within days, they had broken many of Cole's things— a Yosemite mug, a handmade Turkish plate, and a framed picture of his father and his new wife; he'd left it resting on the floor, waiting to be hung. It was evidence of a kind of willful sloppiness.

"They might be punishing you," Daphne said, and

gave him a bag of cat treats called Temptations. For the next week, he filled a finger bowl for them when they visited, and the breakings declined.

Each night of September and October, when everyone was home, the cats moved between the two apartments with almost businesslike regularity. After twenty minutes in Cole's apartment, they trooped back through the cabinet and into Daphne's. Twenty minutes later they were back at Cole's. The noise next door had diminished a bit. The TV was slightly less bombastic, the girls' running slightly less thunderous.

On the first of November, Cole received a tepid invitation to come to his father's house for Thanksgiving, but decided to stay home. Maybe Christmas, he told his father.

A week before Thanksgiving, shortly after midnight, he heard Daphne's side of a phone conversation. It began with hisses and ended in roars. Daphne was arguing with someone; Cole assumed it was the ex. Her ferocity surprised him. The next evening, after he got home from work, she knocked on Cole's door to apologize.

"Stupid ex," she said. "He doesn't check in for

weeks and then wants the girls to come to Nevada for Thanksgiving. He's trying to impress the family of his fiancée—to pretend he's a good dad."

"I didn't hear anything," Cole said.

"You lie," she said, and backed a step toward her own door. "We *are* getting better in general, no?" Her own door was closed, but through it the girls could be heard singing loudly.

"You are getting quieter," Cole said. "But it's never been a problem."

Cole had had an idea that Daphne would ask him to Thanksgiving dinner, though when she didn't, he was both surprised and relieved. The boundaries were clear. They shared the cats, in a way, and shared a wall, and he and the girls exchanged notes occasionally, but otherwise they lived separate lives. Again, it seemed precisely as Cole's mother would have done it. Cole remembered vividly the way she spoke to neighbors—most of them, anyway—from the frame of her front door. Once in a great while she would invite someone in, but she was just as friendly at the front door, where the visits were shorter, the boundaries clear.

He continued to put on his cardigan before greeting Daphne or the girls, and was not upset when he noticed the first streaks of gray in his hair. He was the age of an uncle, and felt he looked like an uncle, and surely the girls saw him as such, as an older man, an older uncle, a great uncle or neighborhood elder. He wanted this—wanted their memories of him to be of a kindly gentleman who lived next door. One day, he saw a rack of reading glasses at Walgreens and bought a pair. He liked the way they looked; or rather, he liked the way they would look through the eyes of the girls. One day, they knocked and offered him a list of unusual foods the cats liked, and he read it through the readers as they grinned up at him.

"Fish heads, I see," he said, and when he was done with the list, he folded the glasses and hung them from his shirt collar. "I thank you kindly."

But the visits never extended beyond their doorways, and this was the way of things until a cold day in December, just before 8 a.m. Cole was in the kitchen when he heard June's voice.

"Mr. Cole?"

He knelt down near the cabinet and instantly Fernando shot through the tunnel and brushed past him, flying into Cole's apartment. He meowed plaintively from the kitchen counter, directing his speech to Cole's ear with great intention.

"You there, Mr. Cole?" June asked.

"Yes," he said through the cabinetry.

"My mama wants to talk to you," June said.

"Okay," Cole said. "Is she there with you?"

"She's at work," June said. "Can I give you my phone?"

June passed her phone through the tunnel.

"Cole?" Daphne said. "I'm at work. My regular carpool can't come today. This other mom is losing her shit. I don't know what it is. Bad meds mixed with edibles, I think. Anyway, my girls need a ride to school."

"Not a problem," Cole said. Fernando was still wailing at him from the kitchen counter.

"Oh god, you saved my life," Daphne said.

"It's so easy, I can drop them on my way to work," he said, though he hadn't planned to go into the office that day. And did Daphne really leave them alone in the morning to lock up? Cole hadn't known this.

"And have you seen Anders?" Daphne asked.

Cole hadn't. Anders hadn't visited for a full day.

"Shit," Daphne said. "Well, keep your eyes peeled. The girls say they didn't let him out. But if he's not in our place or yours, he's outside. Which sucks. But we can worry about it after the kids get to school."

"Got it," he said.

"You're the greatest," she said.

She gave him the address, he put on his cardigan, and minutes later the girls were trying to figure out the seat belts in his Honda. It occurred to him that he'd never had anyone ride in the back seat. He'd driven people in the passenger seat easily eight or nine times, most of his passengers dates, mostly first dates. Finally he heard two clicks and he started the car.

"When does school start?" he asked, and programmed in the address Daphne had given him.

"Eight twenty-five," Savannah said.

It was 8:12 a.m. They would be late. He backed out of the alley. "You want any particular music?" he asked.

"Mama plays KFAB," June said, and Cole tried to find that station.

"It's 97.3," Savannah said.

He turned the dial and found it. It was Top 40.

"You drive slow," Savannah said.

Cole checked. He was going under twenty. Something about having these two tiny, gangly, squirming girls in the car made him cautious, made his car seem very small and fragile. He pictured an eighteen-wheel truck slamming into them from the side. Then a train.

"Are you here for Christmas?" June asked.

"Here in town? Yes," he said.

"What are you doing for it?" she asked. "You can come over. We don't have a tree yet. Do you?"

"Not yet," he said, and up ahead, he saw an object in the road. He slowed down.

"Now you're going extra slow," Savannah said.

The object was an animal. It was not moving. "Oh lord god," Cole said.

It was Anders, killed in mid-stride.

He stopped the car and opened the door. "Don't look," he said to the girls. "Don't let her look," he said to June. "Close your eyes and close hers!"

June obeyed but was already bawling. She'd seen. Savannah had her eyes closed tight.

Cole ran down the road. He held out hope that it was some other animal, but no animal was white like that, not here. It was Anders. Anders had no collar. Cole knelt and looked at him, hoping his own body blocked the girls' view of the cat.

Anders's fur was matted and coarse and dirty, as if a car had idled over him, spewing soot. His eyes were open, his mouth wide in a scream.

Cole's car was parked, still running, in the middle of the street. Did he need to move it? Was that the first thing to do? He ran through the order of operations. First go back to the car. You can't leave the girls in the car. Go to the car, drive the girls home. Then go back and get Anders out of the street. Then get the girls again and take them to school.

Okay, he thought. Okay.

No. He rethought it all. First was Anders. He had to make sure Anders wasn't run over again. So he lifted the cat and immediately recoiled. He was stiff. And lighter than before—a hollow and hard thing with rough and blackened fur.

He thought he might just put Anders under a bush for now. Get him off the street. Cole eyed a shrub but thought of coyotes, rats, raccoons. He didn't want Anders picked at, eaten. He had to cover him up, bring him home. Then get the girls to school.

He took off his cardigan and laid Anders down upon it. He wrapped him and carried him back toward their building. He knew the girls were watching. He couldn't help it. They saw him run toward them and then saw him rushing past, carrying their dead cat before him. So horrible, so horrible, Cole thought. But there was no other way.

And the car was still running in the middle of the street. Shit, he thought. Shit, shit, shit.

He had to park the car and turn it off. He set Anders on the curb for a moment, jumped into the driver's seat. Amid the girls' wailing—they knew it all, had seen it all—he pulled to the side of the road and turned off the car. He jumped out again, got Anders, and speed-walked back to the apartment building. Put him in the apartment? No. He could think of nothing but to put Anders on his doorstep. No one would see him there. There were no neighbors above. He thought to put the welcome mat over the body. The notion was ugly, but the mat would hide him from crows, vultures. And the girls. He could get the girls quickly inside. They wouldn't see the bulge under the mat.

Cole rushed back to the car, got in, and turned on the ignition. The girls were screaming, choking, bawling, clutching at each other.

"I'm so sorry," he said. "I'm so sorry, little ones."

I should take them to school, he thought. They can't help Anders now. They need to go to school. He drove a block toward the school, then stopped.

He decided this was a horror. It was a wounding horror, and they should just let it be terrible and open and raw. He turned to them. Their faces were red, purple, white. "I know this is so awful," he said.

The kids couldn't speak. They were clawing at the doors, the windows. "I'm sorry, so sorry, you two," Cole said, and wondered again if he should take them to school.

He thought he should. He put the car in gear and rolled down the hill and got onto the highway. The kids were crying louder now, and Cole realized that this was madness. They couldn't go to school. How could they sit in class? He turned off the highway, drove home, and parked in the alleyway.

"Where are we going?" Savannah asked.

"I don't want to see Fernando!" June wailed.

"We have to go home," he said. "Let's go home and regroup."

He brought the girls back to their apartment and Savannah used her key to open the door. Cole guarded their view of his doormat. They didn't notice the lump, and ran inside and up to their room. From their kitchen, he called Daphne. There was no answer. He composed a text. *Call me asap*, he wrote, then deleted it. If he were Daphne, he would want all the information at once. *Anders was hit by a car and died*, he wrote. *We found him on the way to school. I am home with the girls. I can stay with them. Call when you are free.* He texted into work to let them know his arrival that day was up in the air. He heard sobbing from above. The girls were in their bedroom, entwined on June's bed.

"I'll stay with you," Cole said. "And when your mom calls we'll ask her about school today." He couldn't get a sense of whether they wanted him in their room, so he made a move to leave. He stood in the doorway. "You two okay alone for now?" Savannah's head was buried under the covers. June nodded.

32

"I'll just be in the kitchen," he said. After his mother died, he and his brother had sat in the kitchen for days, making their way through a case of beer that a neighbor had left on their doorstep. It felt right. They were together, they were near the phone, they were awake. It was a kind of vigil.

So Cole went to Daphne's kitchen, made coffee, and sat. He heard the girls upstairs, and heard them make their way halfway down the stairs, saw them peeking to see if he was still there. "I'm here," he told them. "I'll be here till your mom comes home, okay?"

And they ran back into their room.

But there was still Anders on the landing, under the mat. Cole was grateful the girls hadn't asked where he was. Would they want a burial? He needed a box. He went back to his apartment and found the box his cardigan had come in. He put Anders in the box and the box on his back deck, under a beach chair, and put a towel over it all. He resumed his place in Daphne's kitchen, and she arrived home shortly thereafter.

The girls came back downstairs and they debated going to school. June didn't want to go that day; Savannah did. Daphne turned to Cole.

"They need to go, don't you think?" she asked.

"Whatever you think," he said. He stood and made his way to the door; he'd already been there too long. But she stood in his way and came just short of pressing her hands to his chest to stop him.

"Please tell me what you'd do in my place," she said. "My brain isn't working."

"I'd send them to school," he said.

"Thank you, Mr. Cole," she said, and she packed them into her car and drove off.

Cole helped them bury Anders in a narrow stretch of grass between their building and the condos next door, but the next two weeks brought a new distance between them. The cat tunnel closed one day without explanation, and he saw Fernando no more. The girls, too, were invisible. They sent no notes, did not visit, and Daphne did not call on Cole.

"They'll get over it," she said one night, on the back deck. Cole was watering his plants and Daphne came out to explain. "Right now, though, they associate you with dead Anders. June had a nightmare about you carrying that body, putting it in her face. And we still don't know how he got outside. I'm assuming it was one of the girls but they swear they didn't let him out. So…"

Cole said he understood. He was sure he had not let Anders out, but could not blame the girls.

"It's just a time thing," Daphne said. "They'll be better soon."

It was a week before Christmas, so he asked about their plans for the holiday.

"Nothing much," she said. "Their father is threatening to come visit, so I have that looming. I've insisted he can't come, and I think he heard me."

From the deck, Cole glanced into Daphne's apartment. There was no tree.

"I know the guy who sells trees off the highway," Cole said. "For some reason he's Australian. I can get you one." It was overstepping, but he had nothing to lose. Daphne looked back into her own apartment and winced. She seemed annoyed at how easily Cole could see into her world.

"I can see into yours, too," she said. She nodded over Cole's shoulder and into his own living room. "You don't have a tree either."

"I get mine late," he said. "I was planning to go tomorrow. I can get you one while I'm there."

Cole was lying. He hadn't bought a tree in years. The last time he'd gotten one from the Australian, in a burst of misguided inspiration he'd asked a first date to decorate it with him. They'd met online, her name was Lucia, she made soap. He picked her up, they had a light dinner and then had come to his apartment, where he had the bare tree ready, and four boxes of new orb ornaments in silver and blue. They'd decorated the tree to Nat King Cole while drinking mulled wine, and when they finished, they'd kissed on the couch in the glow of the strung lights. "That was perfect," she'd said when he dropped her off, but in the next days and weeks, she didn't answer his calls or texts. He couldn't understand it.

"They're cheaper and fresher when you buy them later," Cole said. "You want me to grab you one?"

"I can buy my own tree from the Australian," Daphne said. "Are you talking about the vacant lot by the Kia dealership?"

"That's the one," Cole said.

Savannah had appeared behind Daphne. She

peeked out from her mother's hip, eyeing Cole warily. He winked at her. He was now a man in a cardigan who winked at the neighbor-children.

"I don't care if you pay for it," he said. "Just let me make sure he sets aside a good one. I know him. And they deliver for free," he added, though he knew Bruce's deliveries were not free. They were fifty dollars.

It was arranged that Cole would pick out a tree and have it delivered while Daphne was at work. She gave him a spare key, and when the Australian's men brought it in, Cole supervised, making sure they didn't scrape the walls or ceiling.

After they left, Cole turned it around, finding the best side to face outward, and trimmed the lower branches until it looked right. The tree was huge, al- most fifteen feet tall, and looked monumental in their two-story foyer. They would have to add the star to the top by leaning over the balcony railing—a moment he hoped to see. He looked up the stairs, imagining it, and saw Fernando, watching him. Cole would have liked the cat to come down, to be his friend again, but Fernando, too, seemed to associate him with the death of his brother, so Cole didn't bother trying.

When he had finished arranging the tree, he locked the door and went back to his own apartment. He'd bought his own, smaller tree, and had brought it home himself, tied to the roof of his car. He found the boxes of silver and blue orbs, hung them quickly on the tree, and then realized he'd forgotten to string the lights. It was always harder to string the lights after the ornaments were up, so he decided he'd do it another day, or maybe not do it at all. He was sitting on his couch, looking at the unlit tree as the sky outside grew dim, when he heard Daphne and the girls get home. From their exclamations, he could tell that the girls were awed by the size of the tree he'd bought. Seconds later, Daphne was at Cole's door.

"I can't pay for a tree this big," she said, annoyed.

"It's fine. They're all the same price this late in the season," he lied.

"And how much is that?" she asked.

Cole realized that California prices were surely higher than what she was used to.

"Fifty-five dollars," he said, lying again. The cheapest tree they had on the lot was a hundred and twenty dollars. The one Cole had bought for her was double that.

"Good. That's what I'll give you," she said. "Fifty-five. That's about what I budgeted."

She gave him two twenties, a ten, and a five. His new grandfatherly persona would not have taken the money from his neighbor, but he knew he had to.

"It looks nice," she said, her annoyance gone. "Thank you. The girls are gaga. They want to sleep under it tonight."

"I'm glad," he said. "The Australians seem to know Christmas trees." Wanting to free her from further obligation to him, he took a step back into his own apartment.

"Do you want to come in and say hello?" Daphne asked, and tilted her head in the direction of her door. "I think they'd like to see you and thank you."

He followed her into their apartment, and was struck anew by the size of the tree. It looked far taller and wider than when he'd put it there mere hours ago. Maybe it was the scale? Next to it, the girls looked like woodland fairies. They were in their pajamas, lying on their backs under it, staring up into the latticework of bristly boughs.

"Hey you two," he said. "Where's Fernando?"

"He puked again," June said, and sat up. "You wanna see? Mama hasn't cleaned it up yet."

And with that, all was the same again. He sat on the carpet with them and they showed him flags they'd made in school—flags made of felt, representing countries of their own imagining.

"Savannah found a stick that looks like a hand," June said. "Get it, Savannah." And Savannah ran up the stairs to their room and returned with a three-pronged stick that looked not like a hand, but a fork.

"Want to decorate the tree with us?" Daphne asked. "We're waiting until their father sends the ornaments from Nevada. All the ones the girls made over the years. He said they'd get here tomorrow."

"Savannah, get the picture of the tree from last year," June said.

Savannah disappeared again, and returned with a picture of the family, including a wiry, bearded man, in front of a Christmas tree decorated with homemade ornaments.

"Their dad," Daphne said, and pressed her forefinger over the man's face. "Those are the ornaments from when I was a kid, and his, and theirs."

"Wonderful," Cole said.

"Wonderful! Extraordinary!" Savannah said, and June giggled. Cole pretended to be exasperated.

"He's a last-minute kind of person," Daphne said. "But he gets free FedExing at his work, so they should be here."

The next day, the twenty-third, was a Saturday. Throughout the day, the girls knocked on Cole's door, asking if he'd seen the package, if maybe he'd received it by mistake. "No," he said, "but remember that the deliveries come really late these days. They deliver around the clock this time of year."

By ten that night, the ornaments had not arrived. In the morning, Daphne knocked. "Just making sure, but they don't deliver mail on Sundays or Christmas here, right?" she asked.

It was a six-hour drive to his father's house, so Cole got on the road early on Sunday. He turned in to his dad's long driveway in the early afternoon of Christmas Eve. It was a December day in California—crisp and clear and green.

41

Melanie was walking into the house carrying three shopping bags, surrounded by three swirling sheepdogs. She'd dyed her hair a color between white and gold, and was wearing skinny green corduroys tucked into black velvet boots. Hearing his car approach, she stopped, turned, and maintained a showy, confused look for an inordinately long time. Yes, I know, he thought. I've come unannounced.

"Hello!" he said from his car window as he parked. He decided to be breezy and magnanimous, but realized he'd brought nothing for her or for his father. It was Christmas Eve and he'd shown up empty-handed. The dogs leapt upon him, and he hugged Melanie, who still had the shopping bags in her hands. His father had appeared in the doorway. "Is that Cole?" He was shielding his eyes with his hand, though the sky was overcast.

They settled everything in the kitchen. No one sat down. Cole explained that he had a friend who needed Mom's old ornaments, and his father said, "Help yourself, if you can find them." They all agreed that the move to the farm had been chaotic, but if a box like that was anywhere, it would be in the barn. His father found a headlamp in a drawer, tested it, and gave it to Cole. Cole left the two of them in the kitchen, both watching him, looking concerned.

Cole strode quickly to the barn, wanting not to glance back, but feeling Melanie's eyes upon him. When he turned, he saw her standing in the driveway, eyeing him with pity. She had done this for years, her probing, assessing eyes hinting that something was wrong with him, missing for him. He was a forty-four-year-old man, unmarried and living alone, and this gave her—a sixty-year-old who'd never worked, who'd been married twice before marrying Cole's dad—the right of unlimited condescension.

"Thanks!" he yelled to her across the roundabout, and disappeared into the darkness of the barn. He went up the ladder and at the top rung, turned on his headlamp. The light from his forehead swept over a trio of ghostly mannequins in white dresses, the satin shimmering.

He climbed into the loft and, on his knees, probed farther with the light. He saw a rolltop desk, his old drum set, and a coffee table made from sequoia. There were slanting stacks of photo albums, and fading furniture that had been in the house when his father was single. Melanie had moved them. Cole did not begrudge her this. It was generous of her to keep these things at all—to at least allow them to be kept. She could have thrown them away, and Cole's father never would have noticed.

Still, there was a good chance the ornaments were gone. Last he'd seen them, they were in a banker's box, and might have been taken for garbage. If they were gone, he wouldn't say anything to Melanie. It didn't matter. His father was old, and it was not her job to keep the possessions of his dead ex-wife.

Cole stood and probed the space under the pitched roof. A trunk held reams of satin and lace. In the light from the headlamp it was as bright as the moon. He coughed from the dust and directed his white light to the dim corners, throwing parallelogram shadows. There were two clear plastic bins full of clothing, but behind them, he saw the golden surface of his First Communion angel. He crawled into the dark corner and shone the light into this last bin and knew it immediately. He pried off the lid and saw them all, all of the ornaments, all of them preserved, pristine. Some had been wrapped in tissue, some in tiny boxes. Oh! He rested the headlamp on the floor, its light reaching upward, and he laid out the ornaments on the floor, none of them damaged, each casting a long black shadow. Oh! Someone had taken such care!

It was Melanie. Now he knew it. It had to be. His father wouldn't have done it, couldn't have managed it, didn't have that kind of organized mind and tenacity. It was Melanie, and Cole was grateful, and wanted to tell her so. But when he packed the ornaments back into their bin, and lowered himself from the loft and stepped into the light of the driveway again, her car was gone.

Cole went into the house and found his father asleep on a chaise longue, a wool blanket over his lap.

Cole drove back to his apartment, fell asleep at midnight and woke up late on Christmas morning. When he heard the girls pattering around their apartment, he knocked on their door.

Daphne answered. Behind her, he saw the enormous tree, still bare but for the lights they'd strung. On the kitchen counter, the girls had begun crafting ornaments from cardboard and pipe cleaners. They'd cut a picture of Dora the Explorer from the cover of a coloring book and had attached a paper clip to it, a makeshift hook.

"I have some ornaments," he said. "You don't have to use them, of course."

Daphne looked at the bin in his arms.

"Oh Mr. Cole," she said.

"They were mine, my mom's," he said. They were his father's, too, and his brother's, so he didn't know why he said it this way, but he said it and it didn't make sense to correct it. He saw so much of his mother in Daphne that he couldn't look at her just then; it hurt too much; he missed his mother so much, good Christ sometimes it felt so wrong, so searingly unjust that she was gone. He wanted her to meet these girls, too, wanted to walk with her along the water somewhere, have her grab his forearm and tell him something gossipy and delicious, wanted her put her chin in her hand the way she did, tilted, her eyes crinkling, just looking at him as an old friend would—she *was* an old friend, he realized, called him to talk about nothing, and she loved to gossip with him, she had

46

stories about all her friends, her sisters, the clerk at the Ship N Mail, anyone. And after some outrageous little story she'd say, "I mean, there are just no *words*, am I right?" God she was funny.

"Should we lay them on the floor first?" Daphne asked. Cole nodded. It was too soon to speak.

The girls took the ornaments and arranged them in rows on the carpet. They separated orbs, animals, heavy clay ornaments, and handmade projects. There were about a hundred in all, still not enough to cover the enormous tree. But they tried. The girls did the lower boughs, careful to alternate ornament types and to keep the heaviest ones low in case Fernando took an interest.

"Is this you?" June asked, holding up an ornament bearing his picture. He'd made it in third grade. Mrs. Winemuller had had them bring in photos, which they'd glued to orbs and covered with varnish.

"Does it look like me?" he asked.

June brought it next to his face. "I guess," she said, scrunching her nose.

"Your hair was so long," Savannah said. "Was that normal then?" Cole said it was not normal, that he was very *ab*normal, and Savannah laughed.

"Let's put it on the tree," Daphne said, and June put it on a low bough near her.

Cole and Daphne decorated the higher boughs, and to get to the tree's upper reaches the girls climbed the stairs and reached through the gaps in the banister. When they were done, it looked very much like the trees Cole had grown up with. Taller, sparser, but—

"Really the same," he said aloud, then hoped no one had heard him. Daphne, who was on the far side of the room, searching for an electrical outlet, looked his way.

"You say something?" she asked.

He shrugged, no. She plugged the lights in and the tree came alive. He sat down on Daphne's couch, looking at the tree, and thought of a summer trip in the mountains. His father and mother were together then, and his older brother was alive, and the four of them had gone camping in the desert. It must have been Arizona, Cole thought. It had been cold at night, and they'd set up their tents high on a red mountain, and he'd fallen asleep almost immediately after being tucked into his sleeping bag. He'd awoken to his parents making astonished sounds, and poked his head out to see them, sitting together, and above them, the sky's million stars, far brighter than he'd ever seen them, and seeming close enough to flick with a finger. He'd never forgotten that sight, or the terrible feeling of deprivation he had, that he'd never seen the stars like that before. And when they returned to LA, he never saw the stars again, not like that, a night sky that bright. That was the summer his parents began fighting—horrifying battles that raged all over the house, sending him into his room, then the closet of his room, and gave him the resolve to keep his life free of madness, to keep it orderly, rational. His parents had been nuts, his brother went nuts, everyone was so loud and thrashing; he'd chosen a different way.

They finished decorating the tree, and Cole went home. A few times during the day the girls knocked and showed him a gift they'd gotten, and he cursed himself; he hadn't thought to get anything for them or Daphne. They didn't get anything for him, either, so the boundaries between them remained unbreached. In the evening, after sunset, Daphne texted to see if he'd like to see the tree again, on Christmas night and all, in the dark, with the ornaments and lights.

"Remarkable," Cole said when he arrived, and the girls laughed at the word.

"Can we sleep under it?" Savannah asked, and Daphne told her they could. The girls ran up the stairs and returned with sleeping bags, which they arranged under the boughs, and Cole said good night.

"Good night, Mr. Cole," June said.

"Good night, girls," he said.

Cole retired early, and was sitting in bed, watching a show where contestants forged swords from found metal, when he heard the doorbell chime next door. He looked at the clock. It was 9:21. He assumed it was a delivery—the ornaments finally arriving from Nevada. There was no sound next door, though. No one had moved to answer it. The bell rang again, followed by an urgent knocking.

Cole went to his foyer. He heard Daphne's footsteps approach from the other side of the wall, and then stop at her door. She opened it, but Cole heard the tug of the chain.

"You can't just show up," she said.

"Please open the door, Daph," the man demanded.

Cole went upstairs, where a second-floor window allowed him a view of Daphne's front porch. At her door was a boyish man in a shiny winter coat and trucker hat. A jagged bag of presents was resting at his feet. He was wiry like the man in the photo, but had no beard.

Cole was watching from above when the man looked up suddenly and locked eyes with him. It was uncanny; he seemed to have sensed Cole watching. His eyes were like a bird's—sharp and small and quick. Cole retreated from the window, and as stealthily as he could, he made his way downstairs. He got his phone and positioned himself against the wall, as close to Daphne's foyer as possible. He expected a confrontation; he queued up 911.

"Daph," the man said through the closed door. "It's Christmas. The girls should see me."

The man's voice was softer now, even reasonable. They talked for a minute in lower tones; Cole couldn't make out the words. Eventually the door opened.

"Hi peanuts!" the man said loudly.

The girls were awake. They thundered to the door and Cole heard the man murmuring to them. Finally the door closed, and he assumed that the ex had been let inside. Cole followed their sounds to their twin living rooms, and mirrored their movements. The ex's voice was sharp-edged, high-pitched. He whistled at something, and then seemed to tickle the girls. They giggled, ran upstairs, ran back down. Then the sounds diminished. Maybe they were all in Daphne's bedroom? Cole positioned himself on his couch, facing the wall, thumb on his phone. Ten minutes passed, then twenty.

But soon his vigilance seemed unnecessary. The family had been reunited. It was Christmas and he needed to go to bed. He settled in and, for a time, watched his sword-forging show. Eventually he drifted off to a shallow sleep.

He woke to the word "Always!" It had been yelled by the ex, as loud and as crisp as if Cole had uttered the word himself. Shot through with adrenaline, Cole went back to the living room and stood listening, phone in hand.

"Go back to your room!" Daphne yelled, and the girls leaped upstairs. "Leave!" she yelled, and her front door squealed open. Then slammed shut.

"Fucking bitch!" her ex yelled.

She'd tried to push him out, Cole was sure, and he'd thrown the door closed. Trying to signal Daphne, Cole knocked on the wall. She didn't knock back. "Fucking thief!" the husband roared. Then a loud scraping overtook the room, followed by a tinny crash. The tree had slid down the wall she shared with Cole. Daphne's voice spiraled and Cole heard the word "cops," and just when Cole was about to dial the police himself, Daphne's front door opened again and slammed shut, shaking the building. There was a rattle of footsteps on the wooden staircase outside. Cole ran up his stairs and looked out the window in time to see a pickup speeding away.

His phone pinged. A text from Daphne.

Sorry. The ex. Did you hear?

I did, Cole texted. *You ok?*

Fine now. See you in the morning, she wrote.

I'm here if needed, he wrote.

Cole stayed on the second floor, watching for the truck to return. His own parents' fights had had many stages, many acts. One would leave, then return, and the battle would begin again. At some level they must

have wanted it—the thrill of running through a burn-
ing house, surviving, doing it again. That adrenaline
rush of total war. Then his brother, seventeen when
Cole was twelve, had gotten the taste for battle, too.
He fought, screamed, stormed in and out, mixed his
meds with coke and heroin and wine, and was gone at
twenty-two.

Cole waited by the window for half an hour, thinking of how much he hated this chaos, wondering who
would move out, him or Daphne. He could not be
around this kind of madness. He was walking back to
his bedroom when she texted again. *Can you come over?*

"I'm so sorry," Daphne said when she let him in.
The girls were sitting in their pajamas on the couch,
their knees drawn up. The dark mass of the fallen tree
had overtaken the living room like a dead dragon. Its
needles covered the floor, and the ornaments were scat-
tered near and far, most of them broken. Cole's grade-
school face was now in shards under an end table.

"I was thinking we could cut the boughs off,"
Daphne said. "Throw them off the balcony. Then we'd
just have the trunk, and I could help you heave it
over." Cole pictured them lifting the stripped trunk

through the glass doors and tossing it to the muddy ground below.

"Let me see," he said, and lifted the trunk a bit to gauge its weight. It didn't seem so bad. He stepped through the boughs to the top and crouched down until he could put the narrow trunk on his shoulder. Needles cascaded, slid down his shirt and into his shoes. But he stood, and raised the tree onto his shoulder, then inching backward, from the top to the base, pushing it up, up, and heard Savannah's brief gasp as he finally righted the tree.

"What a mess," Daphne said. More ornaments had fallen and the needles were everywhere.

"This broke," Savannah said, and held out a hand-made gingerbread man that had been snapped in half.

Daphne looked at Cole with an expression not un-like Melanie's—a concerned wince that said he should not have lifted the tree, no, it had caused more damage this way, that there was no point, that he and the room were now drenched in needles, and everything was broken anyway so why bother. And that he was a peculiar man, and that there was good reason he was alone, it all made sense why he was alone. But when she spoke her tone was different from the one he heard in his head.

"I can't believe you got it straight again," she said.

"You're all green now," Savannah said.

"Like a big green shedding dog," June said, and Cole reminded himself that he wasn't anything like the troubled, violent man who had wrecked the tree and terrified his daughters. And he was not the hard-drinking man who had ruptured Cole's own family, who had bent and broken his mother and brother and sent Cole into his closet to hide, watching his tiny portable TV and sleeping among the old picture frames and winter clothes. Why couldn't he be the person he'd created for Daphne? Why couldn't he be the steady, slow-moving gentleman next door, in his cardigan and Walgreens readers? He could be that person. He had a right to.

Cole shook his shoulders and the needles fell, tapping like rain on the wrapping paper strewn below. The girls giggled. He shimmied his shoulders, hips, and legs, sending more needles flying, and the girls laughed more, so he did it again, exaggerating the movements, jerking and shaking until they were in hysterics. "You are so weird, Mr. Cole," Savannah finally said, catching her breath. And then Fernando emerged on the stairs above, and languidly walked down, halfway at least, settling on the middle step. Cole hoped Daphne would stay, and that the girls would grow to trust him again, and that the tunnel could be reopened, and that ghostly Fernando would move freely again between the two homes.

Now Daphne was slumped on the couch, smiling, her eyes nearly closed. She surveyed the mess of broken ornaments and said, "I know we should clean all this up tonight, but I'm too tired. I'm gone."

"I'm awake now," Cole said. "I can do it."

"It's fine," she said.

"I know," he said, "but still." And he rose to begin.

ABOUT THE AUTHOR

Dave Eggers is the author of *The Eyes & the Impossible*, winner of the Newbery Medal, *The Museum of Rain*, and *Heroes of the Frontier*, among other books. He is based in the San Francisco Bay Area.

ABOUT THIS SERIES

This short story is part of a larger mosaic called *The Forgetters*, which will, someday, god willing, exist. Its many stories are being released, serial-style but in no particular order, in an effort to confound and delight.

ACKNOWLEDGMENTS

Thank you most of all to Dan. For early reads and astute comments, thank you to Amanda & Frank Uhle, Amy Sumerton, Caitlin Van Dusen, *American Short Fiction*, and of course VV and AV.